AIRPORT ADVENTURE

Written by
Sarah Toast

Cover illustrated by
Eddie Young

Interior illustrated by
Steve Henry

Louis Weber, C.E.O.
Publications International, Ltd.
7373 North Cicero Avenue
Lincolnwood, Illinois 60646

Manufactured in U.S.A.

8 7 6 5 4 3 2 1

ISBN: 0-7853-1067-3

PUBLICATIONS INTERNATIONAL, LTD.
Little Rainbow is a trademark of Publications International, Ltd.

Bump! Ginger's carrier rolls out of the jet's cargo bay. She can't wait to find her family after the long trip. Ginger pushes against the carrier door. It opens!

Ginger bounds out of her carrier and runs straight past the man who refuels the airplane.

"Catch that dog!" he shouts.

Ginger leaps onto a baggage cart. She sits on top of the suitcases piled on the cart. When the cart stops suddenly, Ginger tumbles off.

Ginger jumps onto the moving
conveyor belt that carries baggage. She
rides through the small door with the
suitcases.

The flaps covering the small doorway tickle Ginger's back as she rides through them on the suitcase mover.

"Woof!" Ginger is surprised to see a lot of people looking at her. They are waiting for their suitcases to come by. As Ginger rides around with the suitcases, she looks for her family in the crowd.

A boy notices Ginger. "Can I have that dog?" he asks. But Ginger jumps off the conveyor belt and hurries out of the baggage claim area.

Soon Ginger comes to security. Here
people put their carry-on bags through
X-ray machines so guards can see what
is inside. Then the passengers walk
through metal detectors.

Metal detectors help the guards to be sure the passengers are not taking the wrong things on the airplane. When Ginger dashes through the metal detector, her dog tags set off the alarm.

Ginger runs fast to get away from the alarm. She comes to a room where people watch radar screens. These air traffic controllers keep track of all the

airplanes in the area. They speak to pilots by radio to help them fly and land their airplanes safely.

When one of the air traffic controllers gets up from his radar station to take a break, Ginger jumps onto his desk. Ginger can see most of the airport because the air traffic controllers work in the tall airport tower. She watches an airplane taxi down the runway, then speed up and take off.

Ginger watches another airplane come in for a landing. Then she sees a man near the airport terminal waving orange sticks. The way the man waves the sticks tells the pilot how to drive the airplane and where to park it. But Ginger knows all about sticks. She thinks the man is playing her favorite game.

Ginger wants to play the stick game. She runs out of the tower control room. When she sees an open elevator door, Ginger scoots in the elevator. It isn't long before the door closes and Ginger rides down.

When the door opens again, Ginger smells fresh air. She runs down a hallway and out an open door. Ginger dashes outside to find the man with the orange sticks.

There he is! Ginger races up to him and snatches one of the orange sticks.

"Catch that dog!" shouts another worker, who drops his wrench and chases after Ginger.

Ginger runs with the stick into a huge building where many people are working on a big jet airplane. But Ginger doesn't waste time exploring. She smells food!

A nice mechanic holds out half of his sandwich to Ginger. When Ginger drops the orange stick to gobble the sandwich, the nice mechanic pats her on the head. Ginger licks his hand.

The nice mechanic takes Ginger to the place where traveling animals wait for their families. When Ginger spots her carrier, she runs away from the mechanic.

"Catch that dog!" shouts a worker. But Ginger speeds past him, hurries inside her carrier, then settles down for a nap.

When Ginger's family comes to get her, she is still fast asleep. "Look at our sleepyhead!" Father says.

"Wake up, Ginger," says Mother. "You must be ready to get out and stretch your legs."